P9-CRC-358

MAN GAVE NAMES TO ALL THE ANIMALS

by Bob Dylan

Illustrated by Jim Arnosky

STERLING
New York / London

J.A.

A Note to the Reader

In "Man Gave Names to All the Animals," Bob Dylan has created a song that I think everyone can enjoy singing. From the first time I heard it, the lyrics created pictures in my mind of a land of primeval beauty, where the sky and earth were new, where plants first grew, and the animals knew no fear. I thought this vision would make a dream of a book, and I asked for Bob Dylan's permission to make this dream come true. Happily, he said yes.

Here is the book I envisioned, accompanied by Bob Dylan himself singing his wonderful song. For my part, I have mingled different animals and plants from around the world on each and every page. See if you can match the animals in my paintings with their names listed at the end of this book.

Jim Arnosky

J.A.

Man gave names to all the animals
In the beginning, in the beginning.
Man gave names to all the animals
In the beginning, long time ago.

He saw an animal that liked to growl,
Big furry paws and he liked to howl,
Great big furry back and furry hair.

"Ah, think I'll call it a bear."

Man gave names to all the animals
In the beginning, in the beginning.
Man gave names to all the animals
In the beginning, long time ago.

He saw an animal up on a hill
Chewing up so much grass until she was filled.

He saw milk comin' out but he didn't know how.

"Ah, think I'll call it a COW."

Man gave names to all the animals
In the beginning, in the beginning.
Man gave names to all the animals
In the beginning, long time ago.

J.A.

He saw an animal that liked to snort,
Horns on his head and they weren't too short.

It looked like there wasn't
nothin' that he couldn't pull.

"Ah, think I'll call it a bull."

Man gave names to all the animals
In the beginning, in the beginning.
Man gave names to all the animals
In the beginning, long time ago.

He saw an animal leavin' a muddy trail,

Real dirty face and a curly tail.

He wasn't too small and he wasn't too big.

"Ah, think I'll call it a Pig."

Man gave names to all the animals
In the beginning, in the beginning.
Man gave names to all the animals
In the beginning, long time ago.

Next animal that he did meet

Had wool on his back and hooves on his feet,

Eating grass on a mountainside so steep.

"Ah, think I'll call it a SHEEP."

Man gave names to all the animals
In the beginning, in the beginning.

Man gave names to all the animals

In the beginning, long time ago.

He saw an animal as smooth as glass

Slithering his way through the grass.

Saw him disappear by a tree near a lake . . .

J.A.

Can you find all of these creatures within the pages of this book?
Some appear more than once. All together,
there are more than 170 animals to find!

baby crane
baby swan
bald eagle
bat
black bear
black-necked stilt
brown pelican
buffalo
bull
bumblebee
burro
calf
camel
canvasback duck
caribou
carp
catfish
cheetah
chimpanzee
cockatoo
cow
crocodile
dolphin
dragonfly
elephant
fiddler crab
finch
flamingo
gibbon
giraffe
gorilla
great blue heron
green heron
green parrot
hornbill
horse
howler monkey
ibex
ibis
iguana
jack
jaguar
java monkey
kangaroo
kestrel
kudu
leopard
lion
little blue heron
long nose gar
macaque monkey
mandrill
marsh hawk
monarch butterfly
mountain sheep
mullet
night heron
orangutan
orca
ostrich
owl
peacock bass
penguin
plover
pronghorn
purple gallinule
red macaw
red-tailed hawk
rhinoceros
ring-necked pheasant
rooster
ruby-throated hummingbird
sailfish
salmon
sandhill crane
scissortail
snake
snow goose
sparrow
spider
squirrel monkey
swallow
swallowtail butterfly
swan
tiger
tiger shark
toucan
turkey vulture
vermillion snapper
walrus
white-tailed deer
whooping crane
wild pig
wood duck
woodpecker
zebra

If you need clues, visit www.jimarnosky.com.

To Colleen and Chris.
—J. A.

STERLING and the distinctive Sterling logo are registered trademarks
of Sterling Publishing Co., Inc.

Library of Congress Cataloging-in-Publication Data
Dylan, Bob.
Man gave names to all the animals / by Bob Dylan ;
illustrated by Jim Arnosky.
p. cm.
Summary: Based on a song by Bob Dylan, tells the story of how man
named the animals of the world.
ISBN 978-1-4027-6858-3
1. Children's songs--United States--Texts. [1. Songs. 2.
Animals--Songs and music.] I. Arnosky, Jim, ill. II. Title.
PZ8.3.D985Man 2010
782.42--dc22
[E]
2009030717

Lot#:
2 4 6 8 10 9 7 5 3 1
04/10
Published by Sterling Publishing Co., Inc.
387 Park Avenue South, New York, NY 10016
Text/lyrics © 1979 by Special Rider Music
Illustrations and introduction © 2010 by Jim Arnosky
Distributed in Canada by Sterling Publishing
c/o Canadian Manda Group, 165 Dufferin Street
Toronto, Ontario, Canada M6K 3H6
Distributed in the United Kingdom by GMC Distribution Services
Castle Place, 166 High Street, Lewes, East Sussex, England BN7 1XU
Distributed in Australia by Capricorn Link (Australia) Pty. Ltd.
P.O. Box 704, Windsor, NSW 2756, Australia

Printed in China
All rights reserved.

ISBN 978-1-4027-6858-3

For information about custom editions, special sales, premium and
corporate purchases, please contact Sterling Special Sales
Department at 800-805-5489 or specialsales@sterlingpublishing.com.

Designed by Kate Moll
Calligraphy by Georgia Deaver
The artwork for this book was prepared using pencil and acrylic paints.